Legal & Disclaimer

Legal & Disclaimer

The information contained in this book is not designed to replace or take the place of any form of medicine or professional medical advice. The information in this book has been provided for educational and entertainment purposes only.

The information contained in this book has been compiled from sources deemed reliable, and it is accurate to the best of the Author's knowledge; however, the Author cannot guarantee its accuracy and validity and cannot be held liable for any errors or omissions. Changes are periodically made to this book. You must consult your doctor or get professional medical advice before using any of the suggested remedies, techniques, or information in this book.

Upon using the information contained in this book, you agree to hold harmless the Author from and against any damages, costs, and expenses, including any legal fees potentially resulting from the application of any of the information provided by this guide. This disclaimer applies to any damages or injury caused by the use and application, whether directly or

i

indirectly, of any advice or information presented, whether for breach of contract, tort, negligence, personal injury, criminal intent, or under any other cause of action.

You agree to accept all risks of using the information presented inside this book. You need to consult a professional medical practitioner in order to ensure you are both able and healthy enough to participate in this program.

Table of Contents

Introduction

Life is as diverse as the leaves inside a forest. Each one of us has a story to tell, a message to share, and a lesson to impart. But, no matter what our stories are, they have one thing in common: love. Our love stories may be different, but they share that same feeling of hope when the way ahead seems dark. "Sold: Highest Bidder" is a story of love set in a very uncertain place.

The Book at a Glance

Jason knew he was broken, but it was never a problem. He was contented with his life and his place on earth. What will happen if destiny suddenly changes his mind? What will happen if life sends him someone to make him realize that life is so much more than his little slice of life? Sold: Highest Bidder is a story of hope, above all, it is a story of love. They say that a broken glass can never be repaired. Can one person truly find healing and redemption?

Chapter 1

He knew it was coming, the nightmare. Deep in his sleep, he moved uneasily on his creased bed. It never mattered if he was up on a mountain, out in the sea, or deep in the forest, the nightmare never failed to find him. That night, he saw himself inside a wooden cabin, deep in the jungle of the Amazon. He was enjoying the silence all around him when a door behind the couch opened. It did not have a sound, no foreboding that something was wrong, but he knew something sinister was approaching. He swallowed hard, he knew the nightmare had begun. "No," he said in desperation, "please no."

He tried to wake up but he couldn't. He looked around for anything to hit himself with, but everything began to fade like a moving vehicle being swallowed by the fog. He stood up, aware that everything had disappeared, except for the door. He knew he couldn't avoid it. He had to enter it if he wanted the nightmare to end.

He swallowed hard and turned. It was an ordinary-looking door, only he knew it was not ordinary. It was the door to his past, a past he never wanted to see again yet he is forced to relive most nights in his sleep.

He saw blood. It always started with the appearance of blood, that thick and dark substance he was so familiar with. He closed his eyes and yet he could still see it—the blood of his younger brother.

The door opened wide and the dark shadowy figure of his mother appeared, pleading with him, begging him to enter the room. He looked at her with eyes full of rage. He could hear himself speaking to her without opening his mouth.

"What have you done, mother?" He said to her.

But, as always, his mother only laughed and walked backward to draw the shower curtain. He walked towards her, just so the nightmare would end, and saw there in the bathtub, his brother swimming in the pool of his own blood, lifeless, and beautiful.

Jason woke up in a rage, yelling the name of his brother as loud as he could. The door opened and an elderly man's angry face appeared.

"What the hell was that?" The man said, looking at Jason with a baffled expression.

"Nightmare," Chris, Jason's roommate, said stepping out of the shower.

"Well, keep it down!" The man said in his raspy voice. "Some clients are in the other room, they might think we're killing people down here!"

"Yes, Merkel," Chris replied without looking at their boss.

Jason buried his face in his hands when he heard the door close.

"Here, mate," Chris said, handing Jason a glass of water. "Just another dream, you'll get over it like you always have."

Jason looked at Chris and wanted to explain that he would never get over it, but instead, he sighed, took the glass, and thanked his friend.

The room was almost bare, even the walls were not painted, and it was almost always cold. It looked like a prison cell straight from a third world country prison. The only thing that kept the room from feeling desolate was Jason's paintings. All forty-four of them, in huge frames, piled against the wall like a battalion ready for battle. One unfinished work was propped up on a wooden stand, it has been there for a couple of years now.

"What's Merkel doing down here?" Jason asked after a few minutes.

"A new corporate client from London arrived," Chris replied before putting on his white boxer briefs.

Chris was twenty-eight, eight years older than Jason. They met five years ago in New York, where Merkel found them in an alley, hungry and high as a kite. Chris came from England, where his stepmother forced him to work in New Jersey for a factory that manufactured toys. Chris always thought she did that to get rid of him. Three months after he arrived in America, he ran away after he stabbed his former boss in the eye with a pen when the latter began to make sexual advances on him.

Jason was a very young street artist when they crossed paths. They became fast friends but Jason never told him his story. He never told anyone. Chris only knew that they were both runaways.

5

"Good luck," Jason said, "I'm not working today, planning to go to a gallery downtown."

Just as Jason finished his sentence, the door burst open, it was Merkel again. He stepped inside and winced at the smell of turpentine.

"Why does it always smell like shit in here?" He said, walking towards Jason's bed. "You all right, boy?"

Jason nodded looking away.

"Hey, we have new clients in the house. I want you both to stay put."

"No, not me," Jason protested. "I have an appointment downtown, remember? They promised to buy several paintings."

Blood rushed up Merkel's face, but he kept his cool, Jason was his most prized talent. Jason was the most beautiful young man he had ever handled, and clients loved him.

"Okay, tell you what, kid," Merkel said in a calm voice, "why don't you stay for a few hours, just let the clients see you. I will make sure you won't perform today."

Jason swallowed and nodded.

Merkel smiled. "Chris, you're English right? You are up first, make sure your dick is ready in an hour," he said before leaving the room.

Chris began laughing as soon as the door was shut. "If I didn't know how many girls he fucks in a day, besides his wife, I would really think he fancies you."

Jason smiled and said nothing. He sat on the bed, silent as he always was, and watched his friend put on an expensive suit. "When can I wear one of those?" He wondered to himself. He was never asked to wear suits at work. He was always playing the role of a schoolboy. He was beginning to feel tired of it. He was beginning to get tired of it all. He thought of breaking free but he had no reason to, so he brushed the thought away. Merkel's House of Joy was his only home.

***

Jason stood in front of the mirror, naked. He just took a shower and was about to wear clothes when he took notice of the unfinished painting on the easel. He approached it reverently. He stood in front of it as droplets of water created an illusion that he was sparkling. He lifted his strong arm and gently touched the surface of the canvas. It was supposed to be a painting of his younger brother. The background and the foreground were finished, except for the image of Donny. He could never bring himself to paint him, his childish smile and raised arms pleading for him to pick him up. Jason's jaw tightened, which made him even more handsome. His beautiful and intense eyes trained over his work, a ray of the afternoon sun bathed his muscled chest. He knew he would never be able to finish it.

Stepping away from the painting, he moved his well-chiseled legs towards a rack full of clothes and picked up a random ensemble. He dried himself, including his semi-erect manhood, and prepared to join Chris.

The building on the outside looked like one of New York's many abandoned buildings. But inside, it was full of activity like an ant cave hidden from the real world. Standing in one of the state's poorest neighborhood, the building never attracted any attention. Merkel wanted it hidden because it housed the biggest underground casino in America. It was famous for many other things, but it was most famous for its 'Merkelandia,' a term only insiders know the meaning of. Jason was part of MKD, Merkelandia's nickname. It showcased four shows a night, shows that like the underground casino must be kept secret.

The first show featured a man and a woman, picked from a pool of talents to perform in front of high-profile guests.

The second featured a man and two women.

The third included a woman and two men.

The fourth and last show, 'The MKD Special,' was the last performance of the night. Access was only given to extremely wealthy and very important guests. It featured 'lambs,' men and women, sometimes young girls and boys, kidnapped and forced to do a show where they will end up alone in a room with the guest who purchased them. In special cases, purchased lambs could be taken home by the guest who paid for them.

It came as a shock for Jason the first time he realized what Merkel did for a living. But he soon realized that he felt at home there. Jason knew he was a broken young man. He tried to live a normal life but he always thought he could never fit in. He realized that he hated the world. Merkel made him feel normal, he made him feel that there was nothing wrong with him, and Jason loved it.

Jason never thought he was unhappy there, but at the same time, he never thought he was happy. He was always neither happy nor sad. "Happiness is not for me," he once told Chris after a few rounds of beer one night. "And as long as I am not lonely, I could live with all this," he added. "Happiness always made me nervous, it's always followed by tragedies."

Jason stepped out of the room and began walking along the hallway. It was never dirty, but it had an unhealthy look. He knew something happened when he saw the worried faces of the three Trumpet Girls—Patricia, Andrea, and Camille Trumpet, Merkel's female talents from Oregon.

The three young women approached him and hugged him. He said nothing and saw for himself what was wrong. Chris and a man from the kitchen were wheeling a gurney across the hall, bearing someone covered by a bloodied sheet.

"Who?" Jason asked.

"It's that Russian woman who arrived yesterday," Patricia replied shaking her head.

"That monster!" Andrea hissed.

"The senator?" Jason asked.

No one replied but he looked at their faces and knew it was indeed Senator Perry, their most vicious guest. Three times a year he visited Merkel's House of Joy, which often meant two or three deaths a year. Merkel tolerated it because the senator gave him protection and a vast amount of money. When the senator came, female talents were warned and they never left their rooms. The whole show for the night would then showcase female lambs, never female talents. Merkel knew the senator had a propensity for violence.

***

Jason knocked and Chris opened the iron door. Inside, the man from the kitchen was preparing the incinerator. Jason approached the gurney. He pulled the sheet back and grimaced at what he saw.

"What the hell..." Jason blurted out.

The man from the kitchen gave him a look and Jason stepped back to join Chris, who lit two cigarettes and handed him one. Jason took the cigarette and began to puff. He was taken aback, but he was not shocked at all. He knew all too well that people can be brutal and merciless. He knew that first hand.

"Why? Why can't he just make her suffer and leave her alone when he is finished?" Chris said, watching the flames of the incinerator.

"Why? Well, that's just how some people are," Jason replied.

"He didn't have to kill her."

Jason said nothing and puffed in silence. A moment later, a knock disturbed their thoughts and a voice spoke from behind the door.

"Jason, Chris, the boss wants to see you both upstairs."

Chapter 2

For a first timer, to step upstairs can be overwhelming. The scene was in total contrast with the talent quarters. The walls were lined with gilded paneling and the ceilings with frescoes painted by Italian masters. The floor was covered with French marble, and the whole place was framed by Greek columns.

Casino staff was beginning to crowd the place in preparation for the night's operations. Jason and Chris walked across the space, passing by countless machines and game tables. Some female casino staff could not help but stare at the two extremely good-looking demigods passing by. The women knew who they were, Jason and Chris, they knew they also worked for Merkel, but they had no idea what they did exactly. They were not allowed beyond the casino area and often wondered what was beyond the iron door that led downstairs.

Jason and Chris went up a marble staircase and walked through a long and sweet smelling hallway leading to Merkel's office. An attendant who recognized them opened the door.

"Come in!" Merkel said from behind his desk, holding a handset.

Jason and Chris sat on the couch and waited for Merkel to finish the phone call.

"You met them already, Jason," Merkel began as he placed the handset on the receiver. "The usual group of corporate old ladies looking for some spice of life," he added as he sat on a chair in front of them. "The difference is," he said before lighting a tobacco, "they have enough money to keep this place running for a full year. Chris said one is blue-blooded, our first royal guest."

Merkel looked at them and knew they got what he was trying to say. This new group of clients will be considered a top priority.

"So, what do they want?" Chris said, thinking about the amount of money he could earn. "MKD Special?"

"I don't think so," Merkel replied, " I don't think they will go that far, but they need their fantasy and so we are going to give it to them."

Jason sank on his seat, "Fantasy," he thought to himself, "that meant boyish looks, that meant I will miss my appointment today."

Merkel was eyeing him and said, "Jason, are we gonna have a problem?"

"No, of course not," Jason replied.

Merkel smiled. "I knew I could count on you."

Chris watched Jason nod.

"They don't like the idea of a live show," Merkel began. "They want private shows. Keep in mind that it's the first time that these ladies would be doing something like this."

"Yeah," Chris replied. "We can handle them."

"Good," Merkel replied. "Jason, pick three more—probably Rick, Stanley and James—and ask them to prepare for a long night. I'll take care of the shows for the other guests, both of you will be needed to make sure everything runs smoothly."

"I can help you supervise the shows," Chris said. "Jason can take care of the new clients."

"I will say no more," Merkel said before standing up.

Jason and Chris stood up and left the room.

***

The clients, Chris nicknamed 'Golden Girls,' were still inside 'The Parthenon,' the house's posh restaurant. Merkel could have easily set up an early show for them, but the oldest lady—the leader others simply referred to as Duchess—decided to have tea and an early meal. Jason gave the other talents their room assignments.

Jason was one of the two youngest talents, but he became Merkel's favorite and was easily given the role of supervising the team. Chris never showed it, but he secretly envied Jason. A week after Jason and Chris arrived, the former talent supervisor was dismissed immediately when he punched Jason in the face. That night, Jason assumed his position.

14

Jason never liked the role. He mostly wanted to work in silence and never be bothered by supervising anyone. Chris knew this and took advantage of doing most of Jason's tasks. He was always ready to show everyone, especially Merkel, that he too can supervise operations.

Jason quickly dashed downstairs to change clothes. He was about to open the door to their room when Veronica approached him from behind grabbing his crotch. Veronica, a female talent, was Jason's old fling. Jason turned and quickly opened the door. They stepped inside and Jason pushed Veronica away.

"What are you doing?" Jason asked, perplexed.

She walked towards the bed and sat. She looked at him with eyes full of tears and said, "I'm sorry, I miss you, you never talk to me."

Jason sighed, said nothing, and walked towards his dresser. He began to undress. Wearing only his white boxer briefs, he was looking for something to wear when Veronica knelt and reached for his bulge from behind once again. He was about to stop her when he felt the delicious sensation. He sighed and decided to give in.

"We have thirty minutes," Jason said.

"I only need thirty minutes," she replied before biting Jason's butt.

He turned to face her and let her massage his growing bulge. He could see the excitement in her eyes. He knew she had been thirsting for him for a very long time. She was beautiful, but he knew it would never work out, so he broke it off.

"You like it?" Jason said, smiling.

Veronica could not speak; she was too overwhelmed by what was happening. She spent countless nights dreaming about it. Many times she touched herself in her room thinking about Jason's handsome face next to hers, his strong arms around her, his cock inside her. She missed him so much. Since they last shared a bed, she watched him perform many times and wondered about how he fucked her in the past. She missed being fucked by someone with an angelic face on top of a devilish body.

She removed Jason's underwear and gazed at that massive dick. She smiled and looked up before she swallowed its head. Jason closed his eyes and let himself be pleasured. She licked the tip of his manhood, causing it to grow bigger and stiffer. She stroked it while licking his balls. Jason let out a moan. He looked down, grabbed her hair, held his dick, and asked her to open her mouth wide. In one quick thrust, he forced her to take it. Veronica began to gag.

"You like it?" he asked, watching her face turn red. "This is what you came in here for, right?"

He mouth-fucked her without mercy even when tears began running down her flushed cheeks. Jason then pulled her up and led her to the bed. He

16

parted her legs, revealing her wet pussy. He quickly pulled her panties aside and was about to enter her, when the door burst open. It was Chris.

"Oops! Sorry. Hey mate, the Golden Girls are done eating their dinner. They're on their way upstairs."

"Fuck!"

Jason quickly grabbed a towel and headed to the shower.

***

Jason took a quick bath, and upon stepping out of the shower, he saw Chris fucking Veronica. She was struggling as Chris pushed himself deep inside her.

He ignored them and grabbed one of the only three suits he owned. Merkel would not like it, he preferred him wearing teenage clothes, but he thought that the Golden Girls were a special case.

He left Chris and Veronica and quickly ran upstairs to check the rooms when in the hallway he heard the laughter of women. He turned and saw the Golden Girls walking towards him. They looked like birds with colorful feathers. He smiled and greeted them.

"Good evening ladies," he said, kissing the hand of the one directly front of her.

The old woman blushed showing ridiculously white teeth. "False teeth, of course," Jason thought.

"Welcome to…" Jason started to say when a voice interrupted him.

"He's mine," the voice said from behind the other women.

It was Duchess. The three others moved and made way for her. Jason was impressed by her confident bearing and regal looks. And despite her age, he could tell that she was once a very beautiful woman, in fact, she was still beautiful, still very elegant, and Jason knew what a woman like her required. He bowed low as if he was suddenly standing in front of the Queen of England. Duchess smiled and felt satisfied. Jason took her hand, lifted it, and gave it a gentle kiss.

"The others can find their way," Duchess said in her steady and firm voice. "Show me to our room."

Jason looked past the ladies and saw a figure standing there. It was Merkel, and Jason gave him a nod. Merkel nodded back before approaching the others to show them to their rooms.

***

"This place is not bad at all," Duchess said as they stepped inside their suite.

"Thank you, we are glad you like it."

"That Merkel guy must have hired the best designers. Look at this vase, the same one I saw in Paris when I stayed at The Ritz."

18

Jason hated first timers. He always found it awkward and difficult to guess what they really wanted. Above all, he hated old women, they reminded him of his mother.

"Shall we begin?" He asked.

"Hold your horses, that's not how you start things with me."

"I'm sorry," Jason said, blushing, his handsome face illuminated by expensive lampshades.

Duchess sat on the bed and beckoned for Jason to sit beside her.

"Tell me something about yourself," she said with an elegant smile.

Jason smiled but hated the question. "Fuck you," he thought to himself as he sat down beside her, "I'm not telling you anything."

"I don't know what to say," he replied.

"Tell me about your dreams," she said.

"I'm sorry, but only my body is for sale, not my dreams."

"I could make them come true."

"Did it not occur to you that I hear that all the time?"

Duchess smiled and said, "I am a lonely woman. My husband died two years ago, and my only son in a car crash three months ago. I am the only

19

one left in the family. Two days ago, I decided that money is nothing to me. I can give it all to anyone I choose. I don't care anymore."

"Choose someone else. I don't need your money."

"Is that what you say to the others to get them to give you money?"

He knitted his brows. Duchess saw it and realized that he was saying the truth.

"I'm sorry, I didn't mean to insult you."

"Yeah, so let's get this over with."

"Now, you're insulting me." Duchess stood and faced Jason. "Make me whole again and I'll give you anything you want."

"What do you know about what I want?"

"I know many things."

"Even if that is true, no one can make you whole again but yourself."

Duchess's eyes began to fill with pain and sorrow. She turned her back on him and started to remove her clothes. Jason gazed and admired the beautiful form in front of him. He had to admit, she was the most beautiful old woman he had ever seen. He stood up and helped her undress. He kissed her neck and shoulders. Duchess was quivering, she had never done anything like it before. She had never given herself to someone other than her late husband. The thought of someone new touching her made her both scared and excited. She was conscious of Jason's smooth and firm skin—his youthfulness, and it made her feel a bit embarrassed and envious. She knew she used to be youthful, she used to make men quiver with just her smile, but she also knew that it was all in the past—like a punishment only time can bestow.

Jason cupped her breasts and kissed her lips. She decided to give in, to let go of any self-doubt. She kissed him back. "So delicious," she thought. He began to undress, which made her all the more nervous. Jason stepped back to give her a chance to admire his body. "Is he doing it to mock me?" She asked herself turning to face him. She looked into his eyes and thought otherwise. "Could it be that he likes me too?" She thought. She looked at Jason, his beautiful face, his unbelievable body, and that stiff and massive cock.

She could not help herself, he was the most handsome young man she will ever go to bed with. She stepped towards Jason and knelt, but Jason pulled her up. He kissed her again, tenderly—almost with love—and made her lie down on the bed.

He went on top of her and covered her with intense kisses. She could feel her insides being stirred with joy and excitement. She was not scared anymore. Jason kissed and sucked her neck, cupping her breasts once again. He moved down and swallowed her left nipple. She moaned at the sensation. She could feel his hand moving down, into her hungry pussy. Jason fingered her. She lifted her head and moaned loudly. She smiled, she missed it, her body missed the touch and the attention. "I may be old, but I am still a woman," she thought to herself.

Jason positioned himself between her legs, looking up at her. Duchess could not believe how handsome he was. She could feel her womanhood throb in anticipation. At last, he opened his mouth and ate her.

Chapter 3

Jason collapsed on the bed. Duchess was still gasping for air.

"Get me a glass of water, dear boy," she said to him.

Jason sat up and took a few steps towards a corner table. Duchess could not help but marvel at Jason's youth, that youthful beauty that she sorely missed.

"You are such a beautiful boy," Duchess said, dabbing her face with her handkerchief. "Don't you ever want to get away from this place?"

Jason handed her the glass of water.

"And go where?" Jason answered, joining her on the bed. "I have no family. I have nowhere to go. Even if I want to, I have no reason to. People like me should be hidden."

Duchess watched him speak. She admired his courage.

"But don't you want to be happy?" She asked.

"What makes you think I'm not?"

"Do you owe—what's his name—Merkel, money?"

"I don't owe him anything. I came here out of my own free will."

Duchess could not believe her ears. "How can one freely come to a place like this?" She thought to herself.

"What if I give you a fresh start?" She asked, with her usual elegant smile.

"You mean money?"

Duchess giggled like a school girl and said, "Yes!"

Jason smiled and said, "I have enough money. I don't need much. I need something else."

"And what is that?"

"A reason to leave this place."

"And what can that be?"

Jason shrugged and said, "No one knows, not even me."

Duchess nodded and smiled.

"You are special, Jason. You are. Never forget that."

"You are wrong. I am not special. I am broken."

"I am too. I used to be whole but now I'm not. It would take years to pick up the pieces but time is something I don't have anymore. But, you are still young. You will be able to rise from all this. Go get me my purse."

Duchess watched as Jason got out of the bed. She blushed when she saw his beautiful butt. Jason returned to the bed with her bag. Duchess opened it and handed Jason ten bundles of cold cash.

24

"That's a million dollars," Duchess said with pride. "I am planning to spend all that in the casino later, but I decided it would be better to give it to you."

"But…"

"I won't take no for an answer. There's more where that came from. You may think you don't need money, but you will when you finally find the reason to get out of here, remember that." Duchess caressed Jason's face and added, "You will get out of here. I wish I am younger so we can both get out of our prisons together. But I am old, my days are numbered. The only thing I can do is to help you ensure that you can fly away when your chance comes."

Jason didn't understand it, but his eyes began to fill with tears. He could not explain it. "Who is this woman?" he thought to himself. He touched the tip of her lips and kissed her tenderly. "Thank you," he said to her.

"You may go on with your business," she said with a smile. "I shall sleep for a couple of hours. Can you come back later? Can you accompany me in the casino?"

"Of course," he said, getting up. "I'll wake you up myself."

***

Jason dressed up and went down to his room with the money wrapped inside one of the suite towels. He placed it inside a safe beside his bed.

He was very happy, not because of the money, but because of the old woman's genuine goodness. It was true, he had enough money. He was able to save up over the years, which was easy for him for he never gambled like Chris, never went to dates, and never bought expensive things.

As soon as he closed the safe, he heard a knock.

"Come in!" he said and the door opened. It was Merkel.

"Just spoke to Duchess," he said smiling. "She was very satisfied with you and said that she would return again very soon, good job, boy."

"Thank you," Jason said without a tone.

"Can you help me sort out a new batch of lambs?"

"There's a new batch?"

"Apparently, just the usual stuff, you watch me how it's done."

"Sure, no problem, I just need to take a quick shower."

"Take your time, they won't arrive for another hour."

Jason nodded but felt that there was something else.

"I saw you carrying a bundle of money," Merkel said with a grin.

"What makes you think it was cash I was carrying?"

Merkel laughed. "You would never take anything from our suites. I know I could trust you. I'm just saying that I'm very impressed."

Jason said nothing.

"Okay, I better go. See you in an hour."

***

The van pulled up just as Jason stepped outside. Merkel was already there. Someone poked him from behind. He turned and saw Chris.

"What happened to you?" Jason asked, looking at Chris's face.

"Bloody witches," he whispered to Jason. "They didn't like the others, so they ended up deciding to gang up on me."

"All three of them?"

"Fucking old witches."

Jason gave a hearty laugh. Merkel turned, he rarely heard Jason laugh out loud.

"Boys," Merkel summoned them with a smile. "It's time."

The rear door of the van was opened. Immediately, muffled screams were heard coming from young girls with their eyes blindfolded. They were tourists, kidnapped by Merkel's network of recruiters. Jason was used to the routine.

He saw that there were about six of them inside the van. One caught his eye, the one seated farthest inside the van. A slender figure of a young girl of about eighteen, head bent down. Jason knitted his brows. There was something odd. She was not screaming like the others. It was as if she was resigned to her fate. Jason was waiting for her to look up but an attendant rushed from the building and began yelling.

"Duchess is dead!"

***

Jason rushed to the suite with Chris and Merkel. They found Duchess lying peacefully on the bed, surrounded by her weeping friends and a few security staff.

"We watched the CCTVs," the head of security said. "We found nothing. Thirty minutes after Jason stepped out she began to suffer a heart attack."

"You mean there are videos inside the rooms?" One of the old women said.

"We don't watch any of it unless it is absolutely necessary," the head of security replied.

Jason was stunned. He even felt sad that his new friend passed away. He liked her very much. He swallowed and approached the bed. He looked down at the beautiful old woman lying there. He could still hear her voice and elegant laugh inside his head. He bent down to kiss her forehead before turning to leave the room. The last thing he heard was Merkel ordering the others to stage a scenario somewhere far from the building, where they would fake a death scene just like the others who died inside the premises.

Jason never felt anything like that for a guest. And felt he needed to distract himself or the dark memories of his past would surface and eat him away. He decided to go and check on the new lambs. They need to be prepared for the show the next day.

***

The holding area for the new and old lambs was the most secure place in the building. Only a few members of the staff could enter any time, Jason was one of them.

He ordered the doors opened and he stepped inside the cells. A long corridor appeared before him. The lights were flickering giving the place an eerie look. Moans coming from inside the cells permeated the air and anyone walking in for the first time might even believe that it was the entrance to hell.

"Where are they?" Jason asked the guard.

"4B," the guard answered. "But one was placed in 4C."

"Why?"

"I don't know."

Jason walked towards 4B and peeked inside. The girls were huddled together and they were crying. Jason knew that it was no use, they will be trapped inside for a long time—except if someone buys them and takes them away, which was often much more dangerous.

He stepped away and peeked inside cell 4C. He recognized the girl inside, she was the girl in the van who was surprisingly calm and collected.

"Hello," Jason said in greeting.

The young girl looked up and Jason gasped. She was the most beautiful girl he had ever seen. She must have been European. Her beautiful blue-green eyes were almost luminous.

"Hello," the girl replied.

Jason smiled, she was English, like Chris.

"Can I come in?"

"Do I have a choice?"

Jason felt embarrassed and realized that he was one of the bad guys. He motioned to the guard and the latter pushed a button and the gate of the cell opened.

"Don't move," Jason warned.

"I'm not going anywhere, asshole."

Jason was pleased. "This girl is tougher than I thought," he said to himself.

"What's your name?" He asked.

"What's yours?"

"Jason," he answered, blushing.

"Sasha," she said. "Are you the one who bought me?"

"What do you mean?"

"That's what I heard from the guards, people will come and buy us, like meat in a supermarket."

Jason looked away briefly. He could not take the intensity in Sasha's eyes. He even felt sorry for ever coming.

"No, I'm not the one," Jason began, "but someone will, hopefully, tomorrow night."

"Well, tell those interested that they are buying broken goods."

Jason had to pause upon hearing the word. Broken. "I am also broken," he thought to himself.

"Broken?" Jason asked.

"Yes, broken, wait, if you are not going to buy me, so you must be one of those who abducted me, right?"

31

Jason was taken aback.

"No, I'm not one of those who abducted you," Jason replied shyly.

"Then who the hell are you?"

"I work here, I'm one of…"

"One of?"

"Never mind, it's not important. I just came here to check on you."

"Check on me? Why? Look around, no one can escape this place."

Jason forced a smile.

"Yes, you are right, but I am just wondering why you are not crying like the others?"

"Cry? Should I?"

Jason was lost for words. He also could not help but admire her beauty. She looked like a shy young girl, but there was an intensity in her eyes that he could recognize—that same intensity he always saw when he was looking at himself in the mirror.

Sasha stood up and stretched her arms. Jason could not help but feel his manhood throb.

"So, what is this place?"

"It's kinda hard to explain."

"You can start, I'm not going anywhere."

"Tell me first, you said you were broken, what did you mean by that?"

Sasha smiled and said, "You know what I mean. You are broken too!"

Jason could not take it anymore. He stood up and hurriedly left the cell.

"You cannot fuck with me!" Sasha said after him. "I'm already fucked up!"

Jason ran outside to the parking lot where Sasha's laughter was still ringing inside his head.

Chapter 4

The first show of the month was always the grandest and most exciting. It was a big event in everyone's calendar. Merkel used to hire trustworthy performers from Las Vegas to entertain the guests. Celebrities often came with their wealthy friends, politicians, company owners, tech moguls, anyone with money to spare.

It was a big night for the talents. In one night, they could earn more money than an average person would in one year. It was the perfect time to shine and perform.

Jason performed two shows on stage that night, and one inside the suite. He was tired but very motivated. The shadow of Duchess's death was almost forgotten. He was on his way to the kitchen to get something to eat when he passed by a well-known guest on his way to the MKD Special show.

"Jason, my boy, how are you?" The old man said with a smile.

Jason turned and recognized him.

"Mr. Greene, it's nice to see you again!"

The old man gave Jason a hug.

"I heard there's a new arrival," Mr. Greene said, placing an arm around Jason.

Jason thought of Sasha.

"Yes, they arrived yesterday."

"You done? You're not doing anything?"

"Yes, sir, I'm on my way to the kitchen to get something to eat."

"I'll order something, why don't you join me inside, we'll eat together."

Jason nodded and joined Mr. Greene inside the MKD Special room.

The room was cold. The whole place was carpeted from floor to ceiling. Gilded statues of naked men and women decorated the walls. The audience of less than ten people were seated in luxurious theater chairs custom-made from Italy. Jason sat with Mr. Greene. The small stage looked elegant, above it was professionally positioned led lights and projectors. For the night's show, a Greek-inspired backdrop was in place. The theme of the show was Greek gods and goddesses.

Jason looked around, it was his first time to watch an MKD show from the audience area.

"Enjoying the night, Mr. Greene?" Merkel said, appearing from behind a guest. "I see you're planning to watch the show with Jason."

"Yes, yes, my assistant could not make it tonight," Mr. Greene replied. "I sent him to Australia to represent me. I would not want to enjoy the show alone."

35

Merkel smiled, he saw nothing wrong with it.

"Shall I send dinner for the both of you?" Merkel asked.

"Yes, please, a big meal, my companion here is tired from working all night."

"Jason is my most trusted talent, not to mention the most hardworking."

"He might take your place someday, Merkel."

"Oh, I would not mind that. In fact, I derive much joy in thinking that all these would be safe in Jason's hands. Excuse me, I need to greet the other guests, I'll make sure they send the food before the show begins."

The food arrived. Jason and Mr. Greene was enjoying it when an attendant appeared and handed Mr. Greene a catalog. Inside were the pictures of the show's talents, including the lambs. Mr. Greene was flipping through the pages when he noticed a picture.

"Look at her," Mr. Greene said.

Jason leaned in and saw Nica's picture.

"Veronica, I remember her," Mr. Greene said. "I'm her first customer. I ravaged that small pussy of hers like crazy!"

Jason smiled as Mr. Greene gave out a hearty laugh.

"She begged me to stop," Mr. Greene continued, "but I ignored her of course, a man has to feel the breaking of a woman from time to time."

Jason said nothing and nodded.

"I'm planning to buy a lamb tonight," Mr. Greene said, sipping wine from a crystal glass.

Jason wiped his mouth and said, "Good, we have very good selections tonight."

Mr. Greene nodded. Jason turned and whistled to an attendant and asked for a lighter. The attendant was lighting his cigarette when Mr. Greene noticed another picture.

"I like this one," he said.

Jason puffed and looked at which picture Mr. Greene was referring to. It was Sasha.

"I agree, she's exquisite. What are you planning to do with her?"

Jason hid his surprise, he was not intending to ask.

"I'll bring her to one of my houses in Florida and keep her there forever!"

Mr. Greene gave out another hearty laugh. Jason tried to smile and laugh with him, but he felt weird. He knitted his brows and realized that he cared for Sasha. He puffed and tried to brush the thought away.

"Ladies and gentlemen!" The announcer began. "Welcome to the show!"

The loud music started and a group of dancers from Las Vegas began their opening presentation. Jason knew they had no idea what the rest of the show would be. All they knew about was that it would be a private show for very important guests.

Jason looked ahead and pretended to watch and enjoy the performance. "You are broken like me!" He heard Sasha inside his head.

The show began with two female lambs who arrived the week before. They were drugged of course and didn't know where they were and what was being done to them. Two men, one of them was Chris, stripped their clothes and began fucking them. It lasted for thirty minutes. The next performance happened a few minutes after the first one. A beautiful middle-aged woman with red hair, a female lamb who arrived two days before, her sister was the one killed by the senator.

The last show was announced with cheesy fanfare. Sasha walked on stage on her own. Everyone was astounded, because of her beauty and because she was not drugged like the others. She even smiled at the audience. She was alone on stage when the music began. She lifted her arms and started to dance. Everyone began to whistle, even Merkel was very pleased.

"I like this one," Mr. Greene said, clapping.

Jason watched in silence as Sasha removed her clothes. It was very arousing. It appeared that she had done something like that before. Jason wondered what her story was, where she came from and why could she perform like that.

Fully naked, she jumped from the stage and sat on the lap of a male guest. Everyone cheered and whistled. Merkel sent a signal to the security staff and telling them to be alert. Sasha held the guest by his hair and forced him to suck her nipples. She then pointed at another guest nearby and beckoned him to come closer, then she asked him to finger her. Everyone was wild with anticipation; they had never seen anything like it before.

Sasha's dance lasted for five minutes. Jason could not help but admire her innocent beauty and scorching dance. Merkel gave someone a nod and a male talent went onstage with a whip and handcuff. Sasha screamed when she saw him. A couple of staff members held her and dragged her onstage. Jason stood, concerned for Sasha. He knitted his brows and wondered why she reacted that way when she saw the whip and the handcuff. "Did something happen to her?" He thought.

The room was filled with the sound of her screaming. Mr. Greene stood up.

"Stop it!" He said. "Don't touch her, let the bidding begin! I must be the first to touch her."

"Ladies and Gentlemen," Merkel said, holding a microphone. "Is there anyone else interested to bid?"

The audience went wild, which made Merkel smile.

The bidding began with the first three female lambs. They were sold to three different guests, each for a hundred and fifty-thousand dollars. Jason felt like throwing up. He felt nauseous at the thought of Sasha being driven away and kept as a sex slave forever.

Jason looked ahead. He could tell that Merkel was excited. It was the first time that Jason felt that it might be time to leave the place. During his first month, he tried really hard not to be affected by the brutality of work. But, at that moment he felt that it was finally getting hold of him.

"Please bring out, Sasha," Merkel ordered.

Sasha appeared, struggling with two bulky men in dark uniform. She was spitting at them, kicking them, biting their arms.

"Sasha Anderson, ladies and gentlemen, born in London, eighteen-years-old, abused by her father and uncle," Merkel began. "Not a stranger to straps and whips, as you saw her scream earlier. This beautiful creature can be yours forever! Bidding starts at two hundred thousand dollars!"

There was a collective gasp inside the theater, especially among the men. The starting price was one of the highest ever.

Mr. Greene sat uneasily, Jason could tell he was very excited.

"Two hundred seventy-five-thousand!" Mr. Greene yelled on top of his voice.

Everyone erupted in applause.

"Three hundred thousand dollars!" A man from behind said.

Mr. Greene turned and saw that it was his most bitter business rival. Unable to accept defeat, he yelled, "Three hundred and fifty-thousand dollars!"

Merkel started to laugh in excitement.

"Four hundred!" Mr. Greene's nemesis replied.

"Four hundred fifty!" Mr. Greene answered back.

The audience all stood in anticipation. Jason looked at Sasha, who was standing there in silence and waiting for her fate.

"Do we have another bid?" Merkel said, his eyes filled with greed.

Mr. Greene smiled confidently. Jason turned and saw the rival bidder shake his head.

"Going ones! Twice!" Merkel began.

Jason was shaking, his heart ready to explode. He knew he was not thinking straight, but he was sure of what not to do—to let Sasha be shipped and quietly fade away.

"Five hundred thousand dollars!" Jason said, raising his arm.

Applause nearly drowned out Mr. Greene's protestations. Merkel was stunned and unable to do anything.

"Five hundred fifty-thousand!" Mr. Greene replied, his eyes full of anger and lust.

Everyone was waiting for Jason to answer. Jason looked at Sasha who was confused about what was happening.

"Six hundred!" Jason yelled.

"What's this?" Mr. Greene said in confusion. "Is this a plot to make me bid higher?"

"Six hundred fifty!" Jason said, ignoring his seat mate.

"Six hundred seventy-five!" Mr. Greene replied.

Jason looked at Mr. Greene in the eye. He stood, and towering over the old man, he yelled, "One million!"

Merkel nearly dropped the microphone.

***

Jason opened the door to his room and led Sasha inside.

"You paint?" She asked, looking at his paintings.

"Yes," he said with a smile.

Jason could not believe how beautiful she was, his heart was still beating fast from what had just happened. Everything seemed quiet and he was happy. "This is bad," Jason thought to himself, feeling that something terrible was about to happen.

"These are beautiful!" Sasha said to him with a smile.

Jason's fears disappeared whenever Sasha was smiling at him. He could not explain it. There was a knock on the door.

"Come in!" Jason said.

"It's Merkel, step outside."

Jason and Sasha looked at each other and were very worried. Jason sighed and stepped outside, and to his surprise, Merkel was smiling.

"It was very stupid," Merkel began. "But I admire what you did."

"I'll hand you the money tomorrow," Jason said.

"You don't have to pay me right away."

"I know, but I want to."

"Alright, first thing in the morning."

"So, we're good?"

"Of course we are. I always thought I could see my young self in you. I never thought you would do the same stupid things."

"Wait, you mean…"

"Yep, only I got the missus for a lot less. See you in the morning."

Jason closed the door and could not believe what happened. They were free. Jason rushed to Sasha and hugged her.

"We are two broken pieces," Jason said to her.

Sasha looked up at his handsome face and nodded.

"In the morning we leave," Jason began. "We can start a life somewhere."

Sasha nodded.

"We can go to London if you like," he suggested.

"No, no turning back."

"Okay, we'll buy a ticket to nowhere tomorrow and let's discover where life would take us."

"I like the sound of that."

Jason leaned in to kiss Sasha in the mouth. He had been waiting for this moment.

"What's the matter?" Jason said, sensing that Sasha had stopped kissing him back.

"Oh, nothing, I just realized that this is my first real kiss."

Jason smiled. He looked at Sasha tenderly and noticed tears forming in her eyes.

"Are you sad?"

"No, I'm happy," Sasha replied. "I have never been so happy in my life."

Jason kissed her, this time more intense. Sasha had to break free, Jason was sucking the air out of her lungs. She giggled and teased him. He carried her to the bed.

"My only wish is to make you happy," Jason said looking at her in the eye. "I don't know why, but I feel like that is now my life's mission."

Sasha kissed Jason in the mouth. She began to undress; she could feel Jason was excited. She could feel Jason's erection. She moved so that she could be on top of Jason. She undressed him, slowly, making sure that he had time to wait for what she was about to do.

She unbuttoned his pants to release his manhood. She was shocked at how enormous it was. She held it with both her hands and licked the tip of his dick. Jason moaned at the delicious sensation. Sasha opened her mouth wide and swallowed the head. Jason could feel his dick throbbing while watching her struggling to take it inside her tiny mouth. He always found it erotic when his partners were having a difficult time swallowing him.

Jason pulled her up, and with one quick movement, he removed Sasha's skirt and underwear. Jason stared at her tiny and pinkish pussy. He noticed that it was already swollen out of excitement. He spread her legs wider and began eating her womanhood. Sasha moaned like crazy as Jason

45

expertly licked and sucked her vagina. He stuck his tongue out and tongue-fucked her.

A few moments later, Jason could feel her juice began to ooze. "It's time," he said to himself.

He positioned himself and told Sasha that he was ready to enter her. Sasha knew it would be painful but she nodded all the same.

Jason began to enter her. Sasha started to feel the pressure and prepared herself. Jason slowly, but continuously, slid his dick inside her. He did not stop until every inch was inside Sasha. She started screaming and moaning. Jason's dick throbbed at the sound of her voice.

When his dick was deep inside of her, Jason paused to kiss Sasha in the mouth. She was about to say something when Jason suddenly began pumping her hole. The bed began moving. Jason watched Sasha's face as he pushed himself deeper inside her. He could feel the walls of her vagina pop to accommodate his huge package.

Jason moaned, her vagina was squeezing his dick tight. He could feel Sasha's warm nectar squirt from inside her, filling the hole, lubricating his intense thrusts.

He gathered her legs and raised it high above her so he could fuck her deeper. Sasha could not do anything but submit. Jason then placed her legs on his shoulders. He leaned near her face and with five huge thrust, he released his seeds inside her.

Chapter 5

Jason and Sasha did not get much sleep. In the morning, they got up and decided to get some air. Jason opened the door leading to the parking lot. For him, it still felt weird to hold Sasha by the hand. He never felt like anything like it before. They stepped out, Sasha's hair billowing in the wind. Jason caught her scent, causing his heart to pump faster.

"This way," he said, leading her to a small shade beside the storage area.

It was a beautiful morning. They sat on a bench and watched the activity outside the property from afar. It was as if they were watching a different world in front of them. A world so different in many ways and yet so similar in pain, sufferings, and longing.

"Thank you," Sasha whispered, looking at Jason.

He lifted his arm and touched her chin. He lifted her face and kissed her on the lips. Sasha was delighted, Jason's kisses were never full of lust and shame. She opened her mouth and kissed him back.

***

The car stopped and Senator Perry asked his assistant to go down and get Merkel. After waiting for a few minutes, he stepped out of the vehicle and lit a cigarette. "Nice weather," he thought. He walked a little further and saw from behind a garbage bin, two figures sitting on the bench, kissing.

He squinted and recognized Jason. He waited to see who he was kissing. At last, Sasha broke away from the kiss and gave a hearty laugh, tossing her hair in the wind. Senator Perry's eyes were filled with intense longing.

"Senator," Merkel said from behind. "I wasn't expecting you."

"Merkel, who is that exquisite young lady?" The senator said not taking his eyes off Sasha.

Merkel knitted his brows and stepped forward to see who the senator was referring to. His heart sank when he saw Jason and Sasha.

"That's Sasha, senator," Merkel said before sighing.

The senator turned to look at him and said, "Who is she?"

"She's Jason's girlfriend from Los Angeles, she's here for a brief visit."

The senator looked unamused. He stepped right in front of Merkel with a threatening look and said, "Don't you dare lie to me, Merkel, I can turn this place upside down. I know that outsiders are not allowed in the property, not even your children. Now, I will ask you again, who is she?"

Merkel had no choice. "She's a former lamb. Jason purchased her last night."

The senator smiled and said, "Good, I'll see you inside."

Merkel stood frozen on his spot. He could see Jason and Sasha laughing about something. He shook his head.

"I'm sorry, boy," he said before following the senator inside.

***

"I have never been this happy," Sasha said giving Jason a hug. "Thank you."

Just as Sasha finished her sentence, Jason heard the door opened. He looked up and saw Chris.

"Merkel needs you," he said to Jason. "The senator just arrived, his meeting nearby was canceled and decided to visit."

Jason stood up. Wearing a worried face he said, "Warn the ladies, right away!"

"Relax," Chris replied, looking at Sasha. "I already warned them, everyone is safe."

***

Jason stepped inside Merkel's office. He noticed that his boss looked worried.

"I need to send you and Veronica to buy me some stuff," Merkel began.

"Buy you stuff? Why don't you send one of your people?"

"You are one of my people."

"I'm sorry, that's not what I meant."

"Veronica will tell you what to do," Merkel said, waving his hand.

Jason said nothing and went outside. Veronica was standing there with a somber face.

"Nica, where are we going?"

Veronica was startled and nearly jumped at the voice of Jason.

"Hey, you're here already," Veronica said, forcing a smile.

"Where are we going?" Jason repeated the question.

"Just follow me," she said, walking away.

"I need to tell Sasha…"

"No need, Chris already told her."

Jason nodded and followed her to a waiting car outside.

Half an hour later, Jason looked outside and said, "Are we going to Jersey?"

"Yes, we are picking someone up," Veronica said without looking at him.

"Who?"

"I don't know."

Jason began feeling uneasy, and felt that something was not right. He pulled Veronica's arm.

"Where are we going?"

Veronica's face betrayed her. "The senator," he thought, "Sasha."

"I'm so sorry, Jason, I was jealous."

Jason was furious.

"What have you done?"

"I called the senator."

"Stop the car!"

Jason opened the door and jumped even before the car was able to fully stop.

Jason hailed a cab and returned home, his heart was beating fast. "No, oh God, please no," he kept on thinking.

When he arrived, the place looked quiet as always, but he knew something terrible was happening inside. "No, please, no."

He went inside through a back door. He rushed towards his room, careful not to let anyone see him. He burst open the door but Sasha was not there. He felt like going mad. He collected himself and tried very hard to focus. He needed to find her.

He ran towards Merkel's office, from afar, he knew something had happened. A group of talents was standing outside the office. He saw that some of his female friends were crying.

"What happened?" Jason yelled. "Where is Sasha?"

Chris heard Jason's voice from inside the room and went out to meet him.

"Something terrible had happened," Chris said to him.

"Where is Sasha?"

"She's inside."

Jason walked past Chris, opened the door and went inside Merkel's office. He was shocked to see the senator lying on the floor surrounded by a pool of blood. He also noticed that the senator had a gun in his hand.

He looked around but there was no sign of Sasha.

"Sasha!" He called to her.

He heard a whimper from behind Merkel's desk. He ran and saw Sasha cradling the lifeless body of Merkel.

"He saved me," Sasha kept repeating. "He saved us."

Epilogue

The bus station was teeming with people. They both felt like two castaways in the sea of strangers. People all around them were busy going on with their businesses. Jason wrapped his arm around Sasha, he wanted her to know that everything would be all right. Sasha reciprocated by looking up to kiss his cheek. She never felt so happy in her life. They have decided to go East, to Los Angeles, and if they felt like it, they could go fly to Japan. They had no concrete plans, they just wanted to be together. Anywhere would be fine, as long as they were together. "So this is how it feels like," Jason thought to himself. "To love and be loved."

While walking towards the ticket booth, he could not help but look down and watch the beautiful expression on Sasha's face. She was not perfect, which made her ideal for him, she was broken like him. He bent to kiss her on the forehead. He loved the smell of her hair.

After they bought their tickets, they decided to grab a quick meal. There was a diner nearby and decided to spend their time there while waiting for the bus.

There were a few customers inside the diner. They were serving all sorts of food. Sasha picked a table by the window so they could see the scenery and activities outside. Jason smiled, she was like an excited little girl going on an adventure.

"What would you like to eat?" He asked.

"You decide." She replied with a smile.

Jason could not help but smile back, her smile was very contagious.

A waitress approached them and handed them a menu. From the counter, a customer turned on the television and a news program was broadcasting the senator's death. Heart attack, the news anchor said, claimed the life of the senator. The anchor also added that the senator died in his sleep while traveling to Washington after visiting an orphanage. Jason smiled, he thought of Chris, who was manning the business now for Merkel's wife, "Not bad," he thought, "not bad at all."

Printed in Great Britain
by Amazon